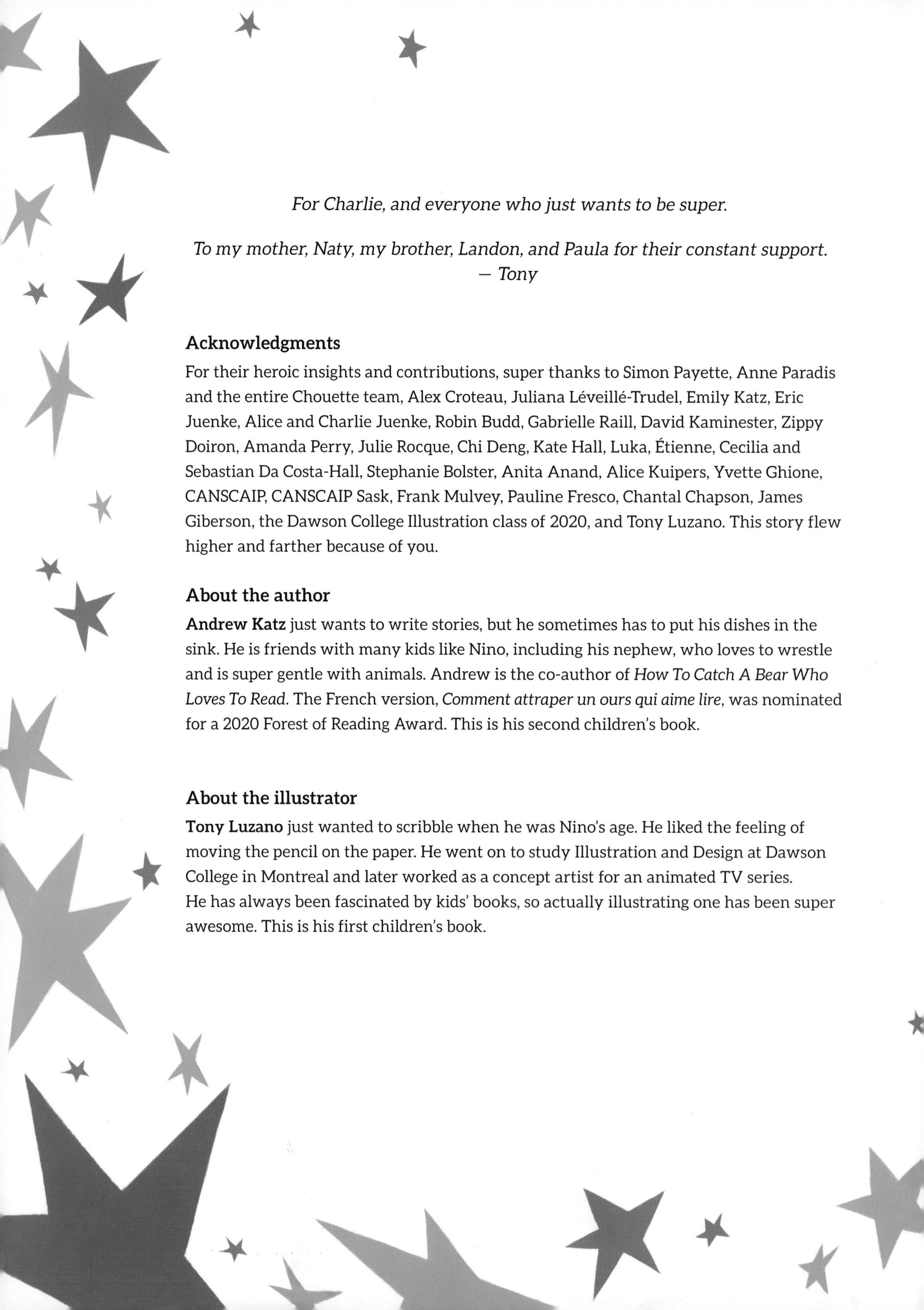

For Charlie, and everyone who just wants to be super.

To my mother, Naty, my brother, Landon, and Paula for their constant support.
— Tony

Acknowledgments

For their heroic insights and contributions, super thanks to Simon Payette, Anne Paradis and the entire Chouette team, Alex Croteau, Juliana Léveillé-Trudel, Emily Katz, Eric Juenke, Alice and Charlie Juenke, Robin Budd, Gabrielle Raill, David Kaminester, Zippy Doiron, Amanda Perry, Julie Rocque, Chi Deng, Kate Hall, Luka, Étienne, Cecilia and Sebastian Da Costa-Hall, Stephanie Bolster, Anita Anand, Alice Kuipers, Yvette Ghione, CANSCAIP, CANSCAIP Sask, Frank Mulvey, Pauline Fresco, Chantal Chapson, James Giberson, the Dawson College Illustration class of 2020, and Tony Luzano. This story flew higher and farther because of you.

About the author

Andrew Katz just wants to write stories, but he sometimes has to put his dishes in the sink. He is friends with many kids like Nino, including his nephew, who loves to wrestle and is super gentle with animals. Andrew is the co-author of *How To Catch A Bear Who Loves To Read*. The French version, *Comment attraper un ours qui aime lire*, was nominated for a 2020 Forest of Reading Award. This is his second children's book.

About the illustrator

Tony Luzano just wanted to scribble when he was Nino's age. He liked the feeling of moving the pencil on the paper. He went on to study Illustration and Design at Dawson College in Montreal and later worked as a concept artist for an animated TV series.
He has always been fascinated by kids' books, so actually illustrating one has been super awesome. This is his first children's book.

I JUST WANT TO BE SUPER!

by Andrew Katz
illustrated by Tony Luzano

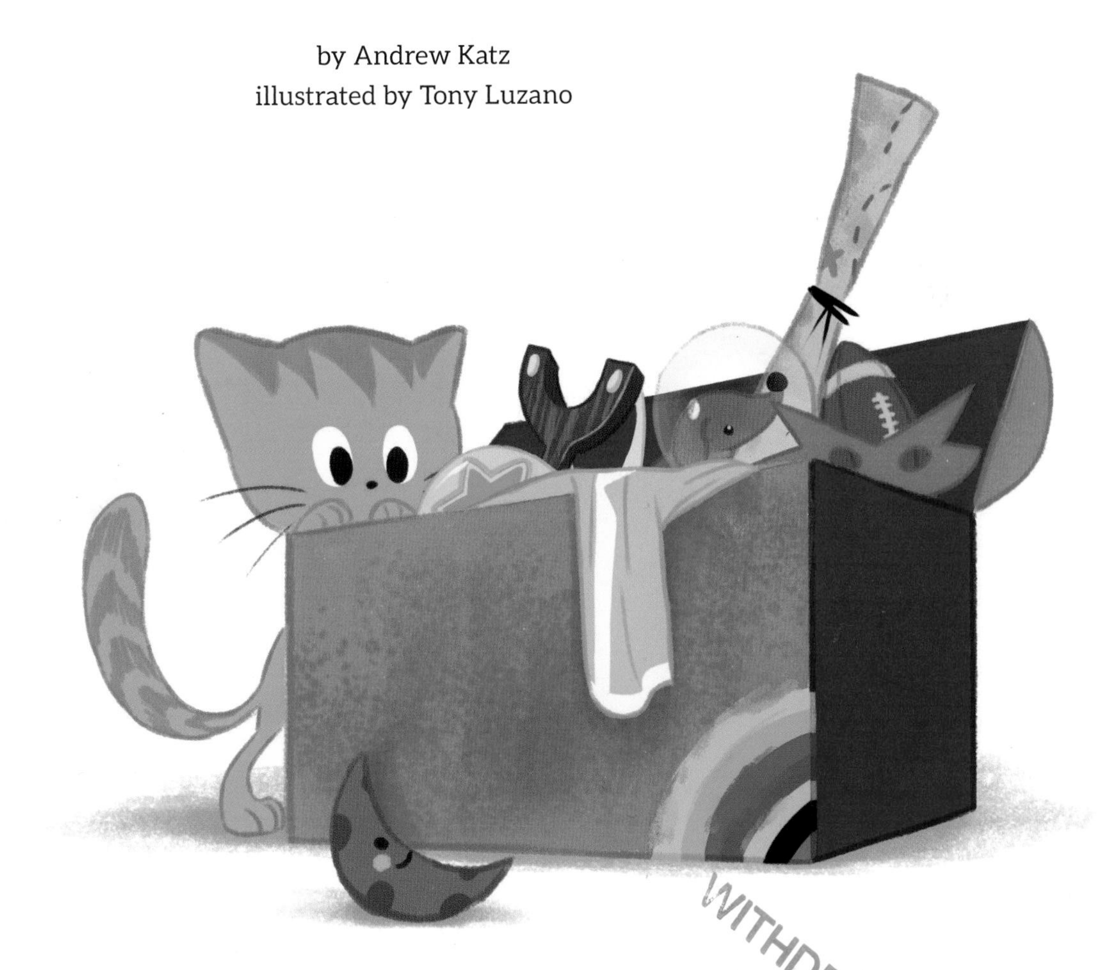

CRACKBOOM!

One morning, Jaguar trotted in carrying something between his teeth.

The mask didn't look like much.
But...

Nino tried it on anyway.

"WOO-HOO!
Look what I can do!"

“Super!” Papa said. “Now please put your dishes in the sink.”
Nino grumbled.
He didn’t want to put his dishes in the sink!

But he did it . . . **SUPER** style.

"Hey Nini!" Liza said. "Want to make a glitter painting?"
"YEAH!"
"Please get dressed before you start playing, sweet boy," Mama said.
Nino groaned.
Getting ready always took forever!

So he **SHAZAMMED** into his shirt and shorts.

Gluing and sprinkling, Nino and Liza made the glittery-est painting ever.

“Anyone want to pick vegetables?” Mama said.
“I DO!”
In a flash, Nino was out the door.

"That's enough tomatoes, sweetie.
We can't eat that many."
"*I* can eat that many!" Nino hollered.
He hurled a tomato all the way
to Hawaii.

Then he sat for a while by a tree.

For lunch, Papa made the world's biggest sandwich.
It was no match for Nino.

During his nap, Nino turned himself invisible
under the blankets.

When he opened his eyes again,
his superpowers were recharged.

"I can lift the couch!"
"Nini, I'm drawing!"
"I can break through this wall!"
"Probably not a good idea, buddy," Papa said.
Nino stomped his foot.

The house shook.
“Why not?!”
“Because the ceiling could fall down.”
“You’re not letting me be SUPER!”
“How about we all be super
in the park?” Mama said.
“WOO-HOO!” Nino shouted.
“LET’S GO-GO-GO!”

Along the path, Nino picked up treasure after treasure.

At the park, he booted the soccer ball with Liza.

Then he spotted a gigantic rock.
"Look! I can throw this rock!"
"No thank you, Nino," Papa said.
"WHY NOT?!"
"You're a super kid. So you need to be super careful. A rock could hurt somebody."

"I JUST WANT TO BE SUPER!!!"
Nino roared.

He blasted into outer space, raced
a rocket ship all the way to Mars,

drank hot cocoa with an alien and
wandered through an asteroid field.
Suddenly, from across the galaxy,
he heard a cry.
MEOOOOOW!

A monster had snatched Jaguar!

The monster was big.

But Nino was **SUPER**.

He wrestled the monster with all his might . . .
until Jaguar was free.

The monster sighed.
Now I have no one to play with.
Nino looked closely at the monster.
It didn't seem so bad after all.
It even seemed . . . kind of super.

"You can still play with Jaguar," Nino said.
"You just have to be super gentle with him.
He's only little."
How do I be super gentle?
"Like this."

PURRRRRRR.
Wow, the monster whispered.

Hey, next time you go to Mars,
could you take me along? I've always
wanted to meet an alien.
Nino smiled.
"Sure!"
The monster raised its arms and
shook them all about.
WOO-HOO!

Nino played outside for the rest of the day.
He shared his treasures with his new friend.
He fed Jaguar supper.

Then he sat super quietly
as Mama read a story.

Nino leaped into bed in a single bound.
Papa pulled up the covers.
"How was your day, buddy?"
As Jaguar curled up beside him, Nino whispered,

"It was super."

CrackBoom! Books is an imprint of Chouette Publishing (1987) Inc.

Text: Andrew Katz

Illustrations: Tony Luzano

Chouette Publishing would like to thank the Government of Canada and SODEC for their financial support.

Bibliothèque et Archives nationales du Québec and Library and Archives Canada cataloguing in publication

Title: I just want to be super! / author, Andrew Katz; illustrator, Tony Luzano.

Names: Katz, Andrew, 1975- author. | Luzano, Tony, 1993- illustrator.

Identifiers: Canadiana 2019003517X | ISBN 9782898021930 (hardcover)

Classification: LCC PS8621.A683 I2 2020 | DDC jC813/.6—dc23

Legal deposit – Bibliothèque et Archives nationales du Québec, 2020.
Legal deposit – Library and Archives Canada, 2020.

CRACKBOOM! BOOKS

1001 Lenoir St., Suite B-238
Montreal, Quebec H4C 2Z6 Canada
crackboombooks.com

Printed in China
10 9 8 7 6 5 4 3 2 1 CHO2091 DEC2019